MARIO'S BIG QUESTION

MARIO'S BIG QUESTION

A Child's Guide: Adoption

By Carolyn Nystrom
Illustrated by Ann Baum

A LION BOOK

Text copyright © 1987 Carolyn Nystrom
This illustrated edition copyright © 1987 Lion Publishing

Published by
Lion Publishing
850 North Grove Avenue, Elgin, Illinois 60120, USA
ISBN 0 7459 2923 0

First edition 1987
This paperback edition 1994

10 9 8 7 6 5 4 3 2 1

Library of Congress Cataloging-in-Publication Data
Nystrom, Carolyn
    Mario's Big Question
    [1. Adoption—Fiction] I. Baum, Ann, ill.
    II. Title.
    PZ7.N996An 1987 [Fic] 86-27770
    ISBN 0-7459-2923-0

Printed and bound in Singapore

This is Mario. Mario lives in a big old farmhouse in the country. It's not a pretty house. It's not even a comfortable house. It's hot in summer and cold in winter. Even the furniture is old, with threads and springs coming out at odd places. But Mario likes his house because it's the kind of place where you don't have to be careful where you put your feet.

Mario's dad teaches history to high school students during the school year. That leaves his summers free to work at home. In summer, Dad plants a big garden full of food: tomatoes and squash and beets and beans and potatoes and onions and pumpkins for pies and sunflowers for birds. Dad teaches all the children to help in the garden. Mario helps too.

Mario's mom works at home. She cleans their big house once a week. She freezes gallon boxes of vegetables from the garden. She washes mountains of laundry in the basement and cooks meals in huge pots on their six burner stove. When Mario's family goes to church on Sunday, they fill up a whole row.

Lots of children live at Mario's house. Some live there for a long time and some for only a few days. But Mario came to stay. Mario got adopted.

A long time ago, Mario came to this big house with its rope swing in the oak tree, six cats in the barn, two dogs in the yard, and a wrap-around porch for Big Wheel races. Mario was only three then. He carried his stuffed dog named Foofee and his blanket full of holes called Geegee.

Mario barely remembers that his first mom carried him up these porch steps, telling him excitedly about his new house. When she gave him a final hug and kiss, Mario felt his cheek wet with her tears. He touched her eye with one finger and said, "Sad?"

SOME children have several different parents. Birth parents are the man and woman who give life to a baby. When a baby begins inside his mother, he is as tiny as a dot on this paper. He is made partly from a birth father and partly from a birth mother.

Foster parents take care of a child who must live away from his birth parents for a while. But foster children usually still belong to the birth parents. Someday they may go back home.

Adoptive parents take a child who has no home into their own family. They give this child the same rights as if he had been born to them.

A social services agency arranges care for children who need a home. Caseworkers from the agency help find foster homes and adoptive homes. Before an adoption is final, caseworkers check to see if the new family is working well together.

Now Mario is ten. Because his family is a foster family, lots of children come and go at his house. But not everyone leaves. Sara and Laura were born to this family. They are in high school now and will live at home until they are grown.

Mario doesn't look like Sara and Laura, or like Mom and Dad either. But he is just as much part of their family. Being adopted means, "I belong."

Mario is not always sure though that he likes belonging to this busy family. If he thinks hard he can almost remember his first mom. When he gets angry at Mom and Dad he thinks that maybe he'd rather be with her.

One Tuesday night, Mario found plenty of reason to get mad. He was sitting at the long kitchen table with his homework while Dad corrected papers for his honors history class and Mom washed the dishes. Mario looked out of the window. The dogs lay snoozing in the backyard sun, which was poised only a foot above the horizon. Mario knew dark would come soon.

Mario couldn't see why anybody needed to know about a dumb war that happened a hundred years ago. So he played with his pencil and looked at the pictures in his book. Finally he folded his paper with a loud slap and said, "Done." Then he scooted out the back door before it got dark.

Ten minutes later Dad stormed to the back porch, social studies book in hand.

"Mario, get in here," he bellowed. "If you did this work, you wrote with invisible ink. How about doing it again with the real stuff? And by the way, since you are so eager to go out instead of do homework, you'll have no more outdoor play the rest of this week!"

Mario felt a red rush of anger building up his back all the way to the top of his head.

"All week?" he yelled. "Just because of one lousy homework assignment?"

14

He grabbed his social studies book and shouted, "I hate social studies. My real mom wouldn't make me do all that work. I know she wouldn't. I want to go live with her!" Then he ran into the house, slammed the door, and ran up to his room.

Mario kicked his waste basket, then he kicked his dresser drawer shut and punched his pillow. Eventually he felt the anger prickles fading from his neck. He gave his pillow a rest behind his back and stared out the window.

"Why did I get so angry?" Mario wondered. Two ideas came to mind: school and his mother—not the mom downstairs peeling apples for tomorrow's pies, but his first mom. It seemed like any time he thought of school or his first mom lately, he got mad. He got mad about school because he never seemed to do as well as Sara and Laura, or even as well as Mom and Dad expected him to. And he got mad about Mom, oh, for a thousand reasons, most of which he couldn't name aloud.

Later that night, Mario's dad climbed the stairs and sat next to Mario on his bed. Mario showed Dad his social studies work that he'd redone—all ready for tomorrow. Dad checked each answer as carefully as he checked his own students' history papers. Then he put his arm around Mario.

"Do you wonder about your first mom sometimes?"

Mario felt a lump in his throat so big that he couldn't talk. He just nodded his head. He wished he could tell his dad the hundred questions that crowded his mind.

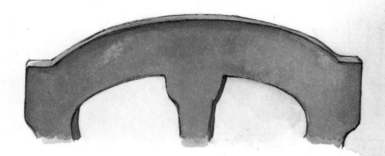

Dad sat still and held him for awhile. But when Mario didn't say anything, he left and closed the door. Mario heard his dad's footsteps get softer down each stair. He looked at the smiling faces of his family in the picture propped up on his dresser. There he stood between Sara and Laura, with Dad's arm on his shoulder and Mom on the other side. But did he really belong in that smiling group?

CHILDREN who are adopted sometimes have a lot of questions about their families. They wonder:

What is my first mother doing now? Does she miss me?

Who was my father before I was born?

Did my first mother have other children? Are they my sisters and brothers?

Who do I look like?

Why did Mom and Dad adopt me?

Do Mom and Dad love the children born to them more than they love me?

Since my first mother gave me away, will my new parents give me away too?

Would my mom and dad feel sad if they knew how much I wonder about my first mom?

Could I find my first mother if I tried? Would she want to see me?

But the biggest question many adopted children ask is, "Why did my first mother give me away?" And behind that question is a nagging crinkle of fear, "Is there something wrong with me?"

Next morning, the questions felt softer in Mario's mind. He took his place at the long kitchen table and bowed his head while Mom thanked God for the food. Mom had made oatmeal with apples and raisins and brown sugar for breakfast—Mario's favorite. Mario looked up and down the long table of assorted children. Except for Sara and Laura with their olive skin and straight black hair, nobody here looked much alike.

Gina was his own age. She had lived with them for six months now, but soon she would go to live with her father and his new wife.

George was living with them just for this school year so he could finish his auto shop course at the high school. Then he would get a job and live on his own.

And banging a spoon noisily on his wooden highchair tray was Jules. Jules' mom had left him alone in their apartment one day and didn't come back. Neighbors brought him to Mario's house. Mom and Dad didn't know how long Jules would be with them.

Mario let his own oatmeal get cold while he helped
feed Jules. Sometimes he made the spoon go round
and round Jules' head like an airplane before he
finally pushed it into his mouth. Then Jules laughed
and clapped his hands for more.

Suddenly the kitchen timer rang and everyone
scurried for jackets and books before running down
the lane to meet the school bus.

"Thanks for the oatmeal, Mom," Mario whispered
as he gave her a quick hug and kiss on the way out
the door.

Maybe being adopted into a family like this wasn't
so bad, he decided, as he ran to catch up with Gina.

21

PEOPLE adopt children for lots of different reasons. But mostly they adopt because they love children and enjoy the job of being a parent. Parents love an adopted child just as they love their own. Sometimes they get angry at each other, like last night when Dad yelled at Mario for lying about his social studies homework. But teaching a child what is right—and then seeing that he does it—is part of the parent job.

Will Mario's parents give him away? No. When parents are thinking of adopting a child, they must take care of him in their home for a long time, maybe even a year. By then they can be sure that they want to keep him until he is grown. Only then can they go to court to sign adoption papers. Once a child is adopted, the law says he belongs to that family just as much as if he were born there.

Wednesday night is family night at Mario's house. Everyone does homework as soon as school is over, and Mom makes an early supper. Nobody watches TV and phone calls have to be short. It is a family time. After supper, they all play games like Monopoly or Ungame or soccer. (Mario likes soccer best.)

Later, Dad opens his Bible and all the kids who are old enough to read use their Bibles too. Together, Mario's family studies a small part of the Bible and talks about ways they can live by what it teaches.

"Tonight I'd like us to look at what the Bible says about one subject: Adoption," Dad began.

Dad didn't look his way, but Mario squirmed anyway. After all, he was the only adopted person in the room. But maybe the Bible would answer some of his questions.

"Did you know that God adopts people into his family?" Dad asked. "Let's see how he does that."

Soon everyone was looking at the first paragraphs of the book of John in the New Testament. Mario listened while George read about Jesus coming to the world. One sentence shot out at him: "Yet to all who received him, to those who believed in his name, he gave the right to be children of God."

Mario's mind stayed stuck on those words. "The right to be a child of God," he thought. "Is that like the right to be a child to Mom and Dad?"

Mario's family talked about the Bible section for awhile.

"It says here that Jesus came to earth so that people can believe and receive him," George said thoughtfully.

"And then they become children of God," Gina announced, with a triumphant look at Mario.

Then Mario spoke up for the first time. "It looks like getting adopted into God's family is just like getting adopted here. It means, 'I belong.'"

By Thursday morning, though, Mario's old questions were back as he stared out the school bus window. "Who do I look like? Certainly not like Sara or Laura or Mom or Dad. I belong with them, but I don't look like them."

Mario tested the shadowy memories of his first mother. He couldn't see her face at all in his mind— everyone seemed big and old when he was only three. Mario touched his own curly hair. Maybe her hair was dark too. Without trying, he realized that his eyes were searching the sidewalk below for a woman with dark curly hair and a face like his. "Maybe if I look every day, I'll find her." But then he thought, "I'd sure feel silly walking up to every dark-haired lady I meet and asking, 'Are you my mother?'"

ADOPTED children often wonder if they look like their birth parents—and sometimes they do. They may even have some of the same talents as their birth parents.

But adopted children become like their adoptive parents too. They learn what their adoptive families teach them. They may even begin to walk and talk and use hand gestures just like their adoptive parents.

Yet one factor is more important than either set of parents: choice. It's tempting for an adopted person to blame everything he does on something he inherited from his birth parents or on something he learned from his adoptive parents. But that's not fair. Almost everything he does, he chooses. And he has to take responsibility for choices himself.

Mario is a mixture of all of these forces. Mario doesn't know it, but his body looks much like his birth father's. But Mario does his homework after school because his adoptive parents have taught him that homework is important. Mario's choices, however, are his own. Mario chose to lie about his social studies. And Mario chose to help feed baby Jules. And Mario even chooses to put catsup on his mashed potatoes.

Thursday dragged for Mario. A faceless dark-haired woman hung in the back of his mind. When school was over, he was trudging out to the school bus when he noticed a woman with dark curly hair. She smiled at him from her blue car. Mario stood still for a moment, half intending to turn in her direction. But then her second grade son jumped into the car, gave her a quick hug, and they drove away.

That evening Mario found his homework boring and supper tasteless. George seemed to notice.

"Hey, Mario," George said, "wanna shoot some buckets?"

But Mario didn't feel like playing basketball. He just shook his head and climbed the stairs to his room.

Then Mario did something he had not done for a long time. He burrowed down into the bottom of his closet and pulled out a bulging pillowcase. Then he sat cross-legged on his bed and emptied the case into his lap. Out fell a tattered blanket and his old friend Foofee. Foofee's right front foot dangled by a thread and stuffing seeped out of a hole in his stomach.

Mario hugged Foofee close. If he held the blanket to his cheek, he could almost smell the apartment where he had lived so long ago with his first mother. He closed his eyes and tried to see her face, but all he could remember were her arms holding him. So he just sat and rocked Foofee for awhile.

A soft tap sounded on his door. Mario started to jam Foofee back into the pillowcase, but not before Mom stuck her head around the door.

"We're making popcorn . . ." she started, then looked at Mario and came quietly over to his bed and sat down. "Do you want to talk about what you are thinking?" Mom asked.

Mario nodded.

"I—I think I miss my other mom," Mario began. He watched Mom's face as she wrinkled her forehead the way she always did when she was worried.

"I mean, I love you and Dad—at least most of the time I do. And I'm glad you adopted me, but I'm scared too. I don't look like Sara or Laura, and I don't do as well in school as they do, either. Do I really belong here?"

Mom had been running her fingers up and down the center of Mario's back the way he liked while she listened. But at Mario's question she slipped her arms around him and held his head next to her shoulder.

"Of course you belong here," she said. Then she was quiet for a moment.

"Have you noticed that your dad and I aren't much like each other either?"

Mario nodded.

"But we chose each other because of love. Then later we chose you—not because you are exactly like us, but because we love you. And just as we choose to keep on loving each other, even when we disagree, we also choose to keep on loving you, even when we have problems."

Mario's eyes strayed to the apple branch outside his window. A lone apple, red and fat from summer sun and rain, waited to be picked before the fall winds blew it to the ground. His mom watched the apple too, but her eyes were distant as if she were remembering something.

"What are you thinking, Mom?" Mario asked.

"I'm thinking," his mom began slowly, "of the time years ago when your dad and I first began talking about whether to adopt a child. We talked about it for a long time. We prayed together about it too. And then you came. Somehow, after that, we often thought of you as a gift from God."

Mario breathed a deep sigh of relief. "Then I do belong," he thought.

Suddenly it felt all right to ask the really hard questions. "But why did my other mom give me away?" he blurted. "Was there something wrong with me? I wonder what kind of person she was—and maybe if I'm that kind of person too?"

"Your dad and I don't know a lot about your first mom," Mom said. "But when you came, we learned a little about her. Maybe we can help you with what we learned then . . ." Mom stopped. "But not now. We need to do some thinking first."

Then she picked up Foofee. "Looks like this guy needs some repair work. Do you want me to stitch him up?"

Mario nodded. He handed Foofee to Mom and carefully stuffed his blanket back into his pillowcase.

PARENTS who adopt children sometimes have mixed feelings about birth parents. Because they love the child they have adopted, they feel thankful to the man and woman who gave the child life and then allowed them to adopt.

But parents who adopt may also feel a little afraid of birth parents. They wonder, "Will my child's first mother come back and try to take my child away?" Birth parents can't do that, because once the adoption is final the child belongs by law to his new family. But the idea is scary anyway.

And parents who adopt may also feel a little worried when they think about birth parents. They think, "What if our child began to love his birth parents so much that he didn't love us anymore?" Then the parents would feel sad.

But even though adoptive parents have these mixed feelings about birth parents, they usually understand if their child asks a lot of questions. Even if they don't know much about these parents from the past, most adoptive parents tell their child what they can.

Friday was a new day for Mario. Even though his talk with Mom hadn't really solved any of his questions about his first parents, Mario felt more settled. On the school bus, he didn't watch out the window for people in the street. Instead, he played magnetic checkers with the boy in the seat next to him. And he even got a B on his social studies test. (Must have been all that hard work on the homework questions.) And supper was great: meat loaf, baked garden potatoes, and apple pie from their apple tree. It was his turn to wash dishes, but Laura volunteered to help.

Afterwards, George went back to school to finish a mechanics project in the school shop. And Mom told Sara and Laura to take Jules outside to play. Suddenly, Mario realized that he was all alone at the kitchen table with Mom and Dad and they both wore their most serious expression.

"Ooops," thought Mario, "I think I'm in trouble."

Dad began. "Mario, you've been asking a lot of questions lately about your first mom and even about your first dad."

Mario gulped and nodded.

"We know that you remember your mom a little, and of course you loved her then. Maybe even now you sometimes miss her."

Mario nodded again. He was glad they understood at least that much. But he didn't know what to say.

"Your mother and I have worked hard to be good parents," Dad went on. "But sometimes we make mistakes. I imagine you can remember some of them, like the time we made Gina eat all her peas and then found out she was sick with the flu." They all three laughed. "All parents are wrong sometimes, so I'm not surprised that you think perhaps you could have gotten a better family somewhere else—maybe even with your first mom."

Mario dropped his eyes to the floor.

Dad continued, "I think most adopted kids ask those kinds of questions. Maybe your first mom knew that too. When you first came to us, she took some time to get to know us. She loved you, you know."

Mario took a deep breath. "So why did she give me away?" he blurted. There it was. The big question lay out on the table between them.

"She didn't want to," Mario's mom joined in. "That's why she kept you for three years. But taking care of you was hard. Your mom was young when you were born, only seventeen. And she wasn't married."

Mario looked from Mom to Dad and back again.

Mom continued. "She tried to make a home for you. She dropped out of school so that she could be with you. But later she could not get a job. So that meant she didn't have enough money for food or a good place to live. After awhile, she began to wonder if she was even being a good mother. It's hard to be a mother when you're not quite grown up yourself."

Mario remembered all the times Sara or Laura had been his babysitter. It was fun for an evening, but he couldn't imagine them taking over as mom every day.

". . . she went to a child care agency." Mario started as he realized Dad had now taken over the conversation. "And that's how you came to us. She especially asked that you go to a home where there were other children and that your new parents teach you about Jesus."

"At first you were our foster child, just like Gina and George and Jules," Mom went on. "But later, your mom decided that she wanted you to grow up in our family. So she asked that we adopt you, and we were so glad."

"I'm glad too," Mario answered. "I think." Then his mind turned to another subject. "What about my dad?" Mario asked. "Do you know anything about him?"

"Only that he was young too, and that he went away to college." Dad stopped as if remembering, then he added, "She did say he was the best soccer player in their school!"

Mario grinned.

MANY adopted children don't know anything about their birth mother or father. But many parents who decide to give their children to another family love their children very much. Giving them away is a hard decision. A woman wants what is best for her child. Finally she decides that her child will have a better life with another family. Her reasons may be much like those of Mario's first mom: no job, no house, no money, no husband.

A child's father may also help decide if the child should be adopted, even if he is not married to the mother. And he too may miss his child when it is gone.

Hard as it may seem, not all parents are able to love their children. They may have been so badly treated themselves when they were young that they have no idea how to love and care for a child of their own. That doesn't mean that there is something wrong with the child—only that he needs a different family where he can learn love. So the child is given to an adoptive family.

It doesn't much matter why a child was adopted. That's all part of the past. More important is the present. Right now, while he is living with his adoptive family, it's best to become as much a part of that family as possible.

Quietly, Mario asked, "What did my first mom look like?"

Mom handed Mario an envelope. "I think you're ready for this," she said.

The envelope was old and crinkled, as if it had spent a long time in the bottom of a drawer. Inside, Mario found a picture and a small curl of dark hair tied with blue yarn. The photo showed a young girl just a little older than Sara. She held a little boy of about three. The boy's chubby arms clung around her neck, their heads close together, each as dark and curly as the other. Was the lock of hair his, or his mother's? It didn't matter.

That night Mario curled up with Foofee. Mom had fixed him so that he wasn't falling apart anymore— just a little crooked in the mended spots.

Before he climbed into bed, Mario put the picture of his first mom right next to last year's Christmas picture of his own family, his real family. Then he laid the curl of hair between them.

Some of his questions had found answers. Some of them would return without answers. Perhaps he would think of new and harder questions. But inside he knew, "This is my family now. This is where I belong."